E $9.96
Th Thompson, Emily
Just like Ernie

DATE DUE			
JY 25 '89	SE 7 '90	JA 16 '92	FEB 0 2 '96
JY 31 '89	FE 22 '91	FE 3 '92	MR 2 2 '95
AG 21 '89	MR 21 '91	MR 9 '92	JUL 05 '95
SE 2 '89	AP 10 '91	AP 17 '92	JAN 23 '96
OC 31 '89	MY 2 '91	MY 6 '92	FEB 0 7 '98
FE 1 '90		MY 16 '92	MAY 16 '98
FE 21 '90	JE 1 '91	JY 13 '92	JUL 16 '98
MR 19 '90	JY 11 '91	JY 30 '92	JUL 3 1 '98
MR 28 '90	JY 16 '91	AUG 6 '92	OCT 17 '98
AP 12 '90	AG 5 '91	SE 12 '92	DEC 0 9 '98
JY 19 '90	AG 21 '91	AP 27 '93	DE 19 02
JY 24 '90	OC 1 0 '91	SE 16 '93	MR 2 1
AG 6 '90	OC 29 '91		

AP 17 '10

Just Like Ernie

CTW
SESAME STREET®
A GROWING-UP BOOK™

Just Like Ernie

By EMILY THOMPSON
Illustrated by TOM COOKE

Featuring Jim Henson's
Sesame Street Muppets

A SESAME STREET/GOLDEN PRESS BOOK

Published by Western Publishing Company, Inc., in conjunction with Children's Television Workshop.

78025

Ernie and Bert are as different as two friends can be. Ernie likes snazzy red sneakers. Bert likes sensible brown-and-white saddle shoes. Ernie likes to play the drums. Bert likes to play dominoes. Bert makes things neat. Ernie makes a mess!

One day Ernie and Bert walked over to the playground to play with their friends.

"Oh, Ernie! Those are terrific sunglasses!" called Grover from the jungle gym.

"Cool jacket, Ernie," said Betty Lou.

"Cowabunga!" said Cookie Monster. "What a lunch box! What's inside?"

Nobody paid any attention to Bert.

"Hey, guys," said Bert, "do you want to see my new paper clip? It's the latest in my paper clip collection."

"Sure, Bert," said Betty Lou as everyone ran off to play tag. "Later."

At lunchtime Ernie told jokes. "Big Bird, why do birds fly south for the winter?" he asked.

"Gee, Ernie," said Big Bird, "I don't know. Why?"

"Because it's too far to walk!" said Ernie. Everyone laughed.

Then Bert told a pigeon joke. "Why did the pigeon cross the road? To get to the other side! Heh heh."

But no one was listening.

On their way home Ernie and Bert stopped at Hooper's Store for a treat. Ernie ordered a Banana-Dana Super Sundae. Bert had a small dish of vanilla ice cream.

Chris and the Alphabeats waved from the next table. "Hey, Ernie," called Chris. "We have a concert today and our drummer is sick. Want to play with us?"

"Sure!" said Ernie.

Bert walked home all alone. "Ernie has all the fun," he thought. "Nobody looks at my paper clips. Nobody laughs at my jokes. It's always Ernie, Ernie, ERNIE!"

Then he had an idea. "I'll make them notice me. I'll be just like Ernie."

The first thing Bert did when he got home was sweep his paper clip collection into a shoe box and shove it under the bed. "Stupid paper clips," he thought.

Then he shook all the coins out of his piggy bank, grabbed his jacket, and took the bus downtown.

Bert stopped at Nickles Department Store, Wally's Drugstore, and Books Are Us.

"I want red ones," he told the salesman at Kenny's Shoe Store, "just like my friend Ernie's."

Later that night as Ernie was looking under the bed for his pajamas, he found Bert's paper clip collection and saddle shoes.

"Gee," he said, "I wonder what this stuff is doing here?

"Hey, Bert," he called. But Bert was already asleep.

Bert was already gone when Ernie woke up the next morning. Ernie rode his tricycle to the playground with Betty Lou.

"Who's that new kid?" asked Betty Lou. She pointed to a tall boy leaning up against the wall.

"That's not a new kid," said Ernie. "That's...BERT!"

"Hey, Bert, old buddy," said Ernie.

"Hey, my man," said Bert. "What's happening?"

"Gee, I don't know," said Ernie. "What happened to you?"

"Oh, this is the new me," answered Bert. "No more boring old buddy Bert. From now on I'm...neato, Ernie, just like you."

Bert followed Ernie over to their friends on the jungle gym, walking just like Ernie. *Squeak, squeak,* went his new sneakers on the pavement. When Bert looked down, his sunglasses fell off and he stepped on them.

"Oh, no!" said Bert.

Ernie picked them up. "Don't worry, Bert," he said. "They're not broken."

But they just weren't the same.

At lunch Bert tried to tell a joke he had learned from his new book.

"Hey, Oscar!" said Bert. "What did one turkey say to the other turkey?"

"What?" said Oscar.

"Uh, uh…" Bert couldn't remember the answer.

"Talk about turkeys," muttered Oscar.

"Better stick to pigeons, old buddy," said Ernie.

Later, at Hooper's Store, Bert ordered a Banana-Dana
Super Sundae just like Ernie. He took a big bite of the
gooey marshmallow, banana, and butterscotch fluff
smothered with whipped cream and nuts. Bert made a
face.

"Yuck!" he said. "Ernie, how can you eat this stuff?"

Back home, Ernie tried to cheer up his friend. "Look what I found under the bed," he said. He pulled out Bert's saddle shoes. "I rescued your paper clips, too."

"I don't want them anymore," said Bert miserably.

"Well," said Ernie, "if you don't want them anymore, I do. May I have them?"

"Er...sure," said Bert.

Ernie carried the paper clips over to his desk, lined them up, and tried to hook them together.

"Ern, what are you doing?" Bert asked.

"I'm making a paper clip chain," said Ernie. "It's not as easy as it looks."

Bert walked up behind his friend. "Ernieee, you're doing it all wrong! Here, let me show you. If you hook them this way..." And Bert began clipping them together like clockwork.

While Bert was fixing the paper clip chain, Ernie put on Bert's saddle shoes. They were much too big for him. *Clunk, clunk*, went Ernie.

Bert turned around. "Ernieee, why are you wearing my shoes?"

"Gee, Bert, you said you didn't want them," said Ernie.

"Ernie," said Bert, "you look silly in my saddle shoes."

"I know, Bert," said Ernie, "just like you look in red high-top sneakers. And listen to us. I clunk and you squeak."

They both laughed.

"We should stick to our own stuff," Bert said to Ernie.
"I don't like sunglasses. I miss my paper clip collection.
It's better for me to be me, and for you to be you."

"Everyone doesn't have to like the same things," said Ernie.

"That's right," said Bert. "Not everyone likes my paper clips, but not everyone likes Oscar's trash or Big Bird's birdseed burgers, either."

"I'll tell you a secret, Bert," whispered Ernie. "Not everyone likes the way I play drums. Chris and the Alphabeats said I play so loudly that no one can hear the music."

Ernie opened a new bottle of Figgy Fizz, and Bert looked longingly at the bottle cap.

"Bert, would you like this bottle cap?" asked Ernie.

"Sure!" said Bert. "Let's make a trade. I'll give you my sunglasses, sneakers, jacket, joke book, and lunch box for that bottle cap. OK?"

Ernie smiled and said, "It's a deal, old buddy."